bobo's
dream

by MARTHA ALEXANDER

THE DIAL PRESS

New York

To David H. F.

&

To Phyllis and Shelly

Copyright © 1970 by Martha Alexander
All rights reserved. Library of Congress Catalog Card Number 73-102825
Printed in the United States of America
First Pied Piper Printing
A Pied Piper Book is a registered trademark of The Dial Press.

BOBO'S DREAM is published in a hardcover edition by
The Dial Press, 1 Dag Hammarskjold Plaza, New York, New York 10017.

ISBN 0-8037-0971-4